Fire Truck Is Flashing

Mandy Archer

Illustrated by Martha Lightfoot

QEB Publishing

The sun rises over the fire station.
Fire Truck waits behind the big red doors.

It is very quiet. Upstairs, the crew is sleeping.

Only Fox keeps one eye open.

The fire alarm starts ringing.

Fox leaps out of bed.

BBBRRRRRIIIIINNG!

Firefighters rush
to put on **boots**
and zip up **coats**.

Fox is first to **slide**
down the pole.

Fire Truck is ready to go!

Hurry, hurry!

Fox grabs his helmet and
climbs into the driver's cab.

Fox flicks **switches** and pulls **levers**.

Fire Trucks's motor starts to **rumble** and **shake**.

The fire station doors **spring open.**
Its lights shine **bright.**

VROOM!
VROOM!

Fire Truck **ZOOMS** out.
This is an **emergency!**

Fire Truck **races** through the streets.

Sirens **wail.**
Red lights
flash.

The **Chief** speaks to Fox on the radio.

NEE-NAW!
NEE-NAW!

There's a **fire** blazing in an apartment building! Fire Truck goes even **faster**.

Fire Truck **screeches** to a stop outside the apartment building.

Flames lick the building and **smoke** billows out.

Fox quickly **unrolls** Fire Truck's hose.

Fox finds a **hydrant** and connects the **hose.**

WWOOOSHH!
A jet of water hits the flames.

The **Chief's car** pulls up.

He points to the top floor—
someone is **stuck inside!**

The crew unfolds Fire Truck's **ladder**. There's not a second to lose!

Fox puts on his **mask** and **air tank**. The smoke will make it hard to breathe.

Fox **climbs** to the top of the **ladder**.

It is **very hot** and there is a lot of **smoke**.

CRACKLE!

CRACKLE!

The **police** holds everyone back to keep them safe.

A woman waves from the top-floor window.

It will be difficult
to reach her.

Fire Truck needs
to move closer.

Fire Truck **edges** back a
little bit. The ladder goes
up again.

Now Fox can reach!

He carefully **breaks** the **glass**
and carries the woman out.

The crowd gives a big cheer!

When the last flame has been put out,
the firefighters put away their
tools and wind up the hose.

The **fire crew** drives back to the station.
It's been a **busy** day!

HONK! HONK!

Fox is very **proud** of Fire Truck!

Let's look at
Fire Truck

Ladders

Water tank

Pump

Hoses

Warning lights

Siren

Storage compartments

Toolbox

Breathing apparatus

Other Emergency Machines

Police car

Emergency helicopter

Ambulance

Police motorbike

For Tamar M. L.

Designer: Plum Pudding Design

Copyright © QEB Publishing 2012

First published in the United States in 2012 by
QEB Publishing, Inc.
3 Wrigley, Suite A
Irvine, CA 92618

www.qed-publishing.co.uk

A CIP record for this book is available from the Library of Congress.

ISBN: 978 1 84835 819 5

Printed in China